LITTLE RED RIDING HOOD

The publication of this book is made possible by a grant from
The Peter Jay Sharp Foundation

A royalty payment for each book sold will be paid to
The Rudolf Steiner School in New York City

First Edition

Published by Bell Pond Books
610 Main Street
Great Barrington, MA 01230
www.steinerbooks.org

Library of Congress Cataloging-in-Publication Data is available.

ISBN 0-88010-571-2

LITTLE RED RIDING HOOD

THE CLASSIC GRIMM'S FAIRY TALE

RETOLD BY CHRISTOPHER BAMFORD

ILLUSTRATED BY PATRICIA DELISA

Bell Pond Books

nce upon a time, a little girl lived in a cozy cottage. She lived with her mother, who loved her very much. In fact, everyone who met the little girl loved her. But most of all her grandmother loved her. She loved her so much that she decided to give her a beautiful riding hood. She made it of the finest red velvet. Her granddaughter liked it so much that she wore it all the time. And so it was that the little girl came to be known as "Little Red Riding Hood."

One day, her mother said to her, "Little Red Riding Hood, carry this piece of cake and this bottle of elderberry wine to your grandmother, who is very sick and weak. They will make her well. Leave now, before it gets too hot. Listen to me carefully! Walk straight to grandmother's cottage. Don't run off the path into the forest – you might drop and break the bottle and your grandmother would get nothing. And when you enter her cottage, mind your manners and don't forget to say, 'Good morning.'"

Her grandmother lived in a cottage deep in the forest about a half hour's walk from the village.

"I will do what you say, Mother," said Little Red Riding Hood, and she set off on her way.

As soon as she entered the forest, she met the wolf. But she did not know what a wicked creature he was, and so she was not afraid of him.

"Good morning, Little Red Riding Hood," said the wolf.

"Thank you kindly, Mr. Wolf," replied Little Red Riding Hood.

"Where are you off to so early in the morning, my dear?" the wolf asked.

"To my grandmother's house," answered Little Red Riding Hood.

"What are you taking her?" asked the wolf.

"Some cake and a bottle of elderberry wine," she replied."

"That's very nice, very nice," the wolf said, eyeing the cake. "And where does your grandmother live, my dear?"

"Oh, a good quarter hour away, under three great oak trees deep in the forest," said Little Red Riding Hood. "You must know where I mean."

The wolf looked at the little girl. His eyes widened. He thought to himself, "What a tender young thing you are, my dear! What a plump and delicious morsel! You'll taste much better than the old woman. If I am cunning enough, I can snap up both of you!"

"WHY NOT LOOK ABOUT Yo

The wolf walked along beside Little Red Riding Hood. After a while, he said, "How beautiful the flowers are! How sweetly the birds sing! But you, my dear, walk along so seriously, with your head down, as if you were going to school. Why not look about you? See how merry and joyful the forest is."

Little Red Riding Hood stopped and looked around. Sunbeams danced through the leaves. Many-colored, sweet-smelling wildflowers covered the forest floor. Fragrant blossoms were everywhere, just waiting to be picked.

"I have an idea," she said to the wolf, "To cheer up my grandmother I'm going to gather a beautiful bouquet of flowers. It's still early. I have plenty of time to get to Grandmother's."

So Little Red Riding Hood left the path and ran
into the forest to look for flowers. Whenever she
picked one, she always thought that she would find
one still more beautiful further on, and so she
wandered deeper and deeper into the forest.

But the wolf went straight
to Grandmother's house
and knocked at the door.

"Who's there," Grandmother cried out.

"Little Red Riding Hood, Grandmother,"
the wolf answered. "I've brought some cake and
some elderberry wine. Please open the door."

"Just lift the latch," Grandmother called out,
"I am too weak and cannot get up."

The wolf lifted the latch. The door flew open.
Without a word, the wolf went straight to
Grandmother's bed and ate her up in a single
mouthful. Then he put on her clothes and her
sleeping-cap, lay down in her bed, drew up the
covers, and drew the curtains around him.

In the forest, Little Red Riding Hood was still gathering flowers. When she had gathered so many that she could not carry one more, she remembered her grandmother and set out on her way again.

When she arrived at the cottage, she was surprised to find the door swinging open. As she walked in, she had a strange feeling. "How odd!" she thought. "I feel afraid today. Usually, I like to visit Grandmother."

"Good morning!" she called out. But there was no reply. So she went to the bed and drew back the curtain. Grandmother lay there with her sleeping-cap pulled down to her eyes. She looked very strange, indeed.

"Oh, Grandmother," Little Red
Riding Hood said, "what great ears you have!"

"The better to hear you with, my dear," came the reply.

"Oh, Grandmother," she said, "what great eyes you have!"
"The better to see you with, my dear."

"Oh, grandmother, what great hands you have!"
exclaimed Little Red Riding Hood.

"The better to grab you with, my dear," growled the voice.

Oh, grandmother, what a horrible, great snout you have!"
Little Red Riding Hood cried out.

"The better to eat you with!" said the wolf.
And he sprang out of bed and, in one bite, gobbled her up.

No sooner had he finished than he felt very full,
so he lay down in the bed, and fell fast asleep.
Soon, he was snoring loudly.

Just then, the hunter was passing by the cottage
and heard the snores. He thought to himself,
"How loudly that old woman snores! I must see if
anything is wrong."

Entering the cottage, he saw the wolf
lying fast asleep in the bed and cried
out, "So there you are, you old rogue!
I have been looking for you for a long,
long time."

He aimed his gun at the wolf, and was about to shoot. Then
he realized that the wolf had eaten the grandmother and he
might still be able to save her. He put down his gun and,
taking a pair of scissors, began to cut open the sleeping wolf's
belly. After the first few cuts, he saw a little red hood. He cut
a little more, and Little Red Riding Hood jumped out. "How
frightened I was!" she cried. "It was so dark inside the wolf."

Grandmother was just behind her. She was alive, but she could hardly breathe. Then Little Red Riding Hood fetched some big stones, and they put them into the wolf's belly. When he woke up and tried to run away, the stones were so heavy that he fell to the ground dead! Now all three were very happy.

Now all three were very happy.

The hunter skinned the wolf, took the fur, and went home
with it. Grandmother ate the cake and drank the wine and
grew strong and healthy again. And Little Red Riding Hood
said to herself, "I will never wander from the forest path
after my mother has told me not to!"

COMMENTARY

long with the Bible and Shakespeare, the fairy tales of the Brothers Grimm rank among the most read works of the Western world. While philosophies, artistic styles and religious conventions have changed over the decades, these tales have endured through the centuries. *Little Red Riding Hood* is perhaps the best known story of this collection. What accounts for this popularity? As in all of the Grimm fairy tales, the characters in this story can lead us to discover treasures in our own souls. Yet, in our modern age, with its emphasis on science and technology, the wolf's speaking and his eating the old grandmother and Red Riding Hood appear to be drawn from the depths of a remote and superstitious past. More imaginative readers, however, like Goethe, Rudolf Steiner, C. G. Jung, and Bruno Bettelheim have always recognized that fairy tales are not to be judged on the scales of science and reason. They know that there is deep meaning and wisdom in all genuine fairy tales—no matter how absurd or grotesque they may appear to us today. Rather, as the German poet Novalis wrote, "They are prophetic, idealistic and inevitable, all in one."

However deep their meaning, fairy tales should be told to children without any explanation. Children unite quite naturally with the inner significance of the stories. They absorb the language of the imagination naturally and feel intimately related to it. Interpretation is unnecessary and would be quite a mistake. Emotionally involved with a given tale, the young child's imagination should not be disturbed.

For the teacher or the parent it is very worthwhile to gain knowledge of the psychological and spiritual qualities underlying the story, for they can then tell or read the tale to the child with conviction.

airy tales can be interpreted in as many ways as there are interpreters. Reading the literature one finds a large array of explanations ranging from the literal to the psychological, the religious and the spiritual. The present brief commentary attempts to be concise but comprehensive in its approach.

At first glance *Little Red Riding Hood (Little Red Riding Cap)* seems like such a simple story. But, to begin with, its time, place and experiences are not to be understood in a literal way. The tale takes place in inner time, not specific time, as indicated by the very familiar "Once upon a time…." It takes place in a world of imagination, in which a child is completely at home. Furthermore, it takes place in inner space with no specific locations. It is "home," "forest," "mother" and "grandmother's house." The experiences—like the meeting with the wolf, being devoured by the animal and being saved by the hunter—are also of a very important inner nature.

In the late Middle Ages, fairy tales became the peoples' mode of relating to Biblical truths. Intensely responsive to images and feelings, medieval folk embraced fairy tales as messages from the spiritual world, second only in importance to the Bible itself. The original meaning of the German word for fairy tales is "messages." These stories are also tales of destiny, our destiny. The word "fairy" derives from the Latin "fata," meaning "the Fates"—those who weave our destiny.

What message of destiny is conveyed by *Little Red Riding Hood*?

As in any great work of art, many layers of meaning can be found in this, or any true fairy tale. To begin with, consider the red colored riding hood. Red is the color of the heart, the blood. It stands for both love and courage. In times past, the head covering worn by a human being had a definite significance. It expressed an individual's status or the class to which he or she belonged. A remnant of this tradition may be seen in the mortarboard of a university graduate. Here, too, a sign set upon the head denotes a particular rank or quality. So, even in the title of the tale, there are meanings that have to do with love, courage, and the role in the world in which we find ourselves.

The next image we have is the errand that the mother entrusts to her child. She is to take a piece of cake and a bottle of wine to her ill and weak grandmother. In many fairy tales, errands and journeys are a prominent part of the story and represent our life journey itself. In this particular case, the task involves the ancient symbols of bread and wine.

In both the Old and New Testaments, partaking of bread and wine has great significance. Melchizedek, King of Salem, in Genesis 14:18, brought these gifts in his meeting with Abram (Abraham). In the New Testament bread and wine are the symbols of the Holy Communion. The word "communion" has the meaning of a close and healing spiritual relationship. And it is to *heal* her grandmother that Red Riding Hood is sent on her journey. She, the new, is to heal the old, her grandmother.

It is important to understand that the change from the old to the new is the very essence of the story of the evolution of humanity—the passage from one generation to another. As we evolve into the future, everything depends on the maturing of the individual sense of self. But to achieve such individuation, we undergo many trials and tests. We must learn to develop our own powers.

The mother knows of these dangers to which the soul is exposed when it sets out on such a path leading into the future. She also intends that the past (in the symbol of the grandmother) should be reconciled and healed. She trusts that her impressive warning will suffice to keep the child on the right path. But, as with many a youth, advice from our elders is not enough. Once the protection of the mother has been removed and the child is on her own, all is changed.

It is in the nature of almost any trial undergone by a human being that he or she is alone in it. Each of us may receive help, but initially we must be alone, thrown upon our resources. In a fairy tale, the forest is almost always the context in which the soul awakens to inner perception. Two other very well-known examples of the forest experience are found in *Hansel and Gretel* and *Snow White*.

When the human being does reach this real world of imagination – comes into the "forest"– then he or she is exposed to great dangers. These are the trials through which a person has to go on the path of spiritual development. When the hindering powers come to meet the person they appear in animal forms before the soul. In the case of Red Riding Hood, the animal encountered is the wolf: the covetous, grasping, insatiable being that drives the human being greedily through life. Red Riding Hood is quite unprepared for such a meeting and in her innocence does not recognize the wickedness of this being.

One must recognize an adversary in order to meet it successfully. In contrast to this, Red Riding Hood trusts the wolf, which at once shows its superiority: It knows the child's particular weakness and makes use of it.

The temptation that the wolf uses to trick the child is familiar to all of us – the pleasures of the world. The more we tame the animal within us, the less we are susceptible to these temptations. In the case of Little Red Riding Hood, she cannot resist the wolf's suggestion to go off the path to pick the beautiful flowers. The wolf is able to go ahead and eat the grandmother and wait for the tardy child to come later.

When Red Riding Hood finally reaches her destination, she begins the slow process of becoming aware. She makes three observations, indicating some concern about the wolf in disguise. But even with the third one, "what great hands you have!" she doesn't use the word "paws." It is only with the fourth one that Little Red Riding Hood becomes awakened with "Oh, grandmother, what a horrible, great snout you have!" The child finally sees that she is facing an animal and not her grandmother. There is no mistaking the snout for a human mouth. The recognition is too late. The wolf devours the child in an archetypical picture of the soul meeting the adversary of the lower self.

Again and again in myths and fairy tales the human being undergoes great trials, whether with a wolf; a giant, as in Jack and the beanstalk; or a great whale, as happened to Jonah. Red Riding Hood and the grandmother have to go through the dark time of utter despair before they can be saved. But to be awakened to a higher stage of consciousness they need true help, and such help in the image of the hunter now approaches. The hunter in a fairy tale is always

of a special significance. He is often a determining factor in the destiny of the beings in the story. He is also there for Snow White, and in many other tales. And is is the hunter who, just before is is too late, saves Little Red Riding Hood and her grandmother.

The clear elevated consciousness of the hunter is indicated with another symbol: He uses scissors to cut open the belly of the wolf. Scissors are always a sign of cleverness in a fairy tale. Upon being freed, Little Red Riding Hood shows that she has learned from her terrifying experience by putting an end to the evil forces that have seduced her. She fills the wolf's belly with stones, so that he sinks to the ground and falls down dead. The grandmother eats the cake and drinks the wine and recovers her strength.

The fairy tale *Little Red Riding Hood* describes the journey to spiritual self-awareness in a most wonderful way. In their vivid imagination children experience the great truths in this story. It is for us as adults to regain this experience and appreciate it too.

ANDREW FLAXMAN, graduated *cum laude* from Princeton and earned a master's degree in business at Rutgers. After a successful career as an investment banker and stockbroker, he turned his focus to educational activities. Presently he is Director of Educate Yourself for Tomorrow, an on-line Liberal Arts program, and Director of Development at SteinerBooks.

For more information on the wisdom of fairy tales read *The Wisdom of Fairy Tales* by Rudolf Meyer (Floris Books, Anthroposophic Press, London, 1988).

For a detailed interpretation of *Little Red Riding Hood* see the booklet by N.Glas (Education and Science Publications, Great Britain, 1947).

For a Freudian discussion of fairy tales see *The Uses of Enchantment – The Meaning and Importance of Fairy Tales* by Bruno Bettelheim (Vintage Books, New York, 1989).

For a Jungian discussion of fairy tales see *The Interpretation of Fairy Tales* by Marie-Louise Von Franz (Shambhala, Boston & London, 1996).

"I will never wander from the forest path
after my mother has told me not to!"